Written by Sarah Glasscock
Illustrated by D. R. Greenlaw

STECK-VAUGHN
ELEMENTARY · SECONDARY · ADULT · LIBRARY
A Harcourt Classroom Education Company

www.steck-vaughn.com

Contents

A River in Trouble

It was the year 2097. Vince was floating on his back in the clear water of the San Carlos River. His computer named Jane was waving from the shore.

"Jane, would you show me what this river looked like one hundred years ago?" Vince asked.

"Sure. Why do you want to see it as it was back then?" asked Jane.

"I'd just like to know if the river was this beautiful then," said Vince.

Soon Jane's screen lit up. There was a picture of the river as it had looked one hundred years ago. Jane made the picture bigger so Vince could see it.

Vince looked closely and saw a man and his son fishing. "Maybe that's my great-great grandfather!"

Jane quickly searched her computer memory. "That could be. You did have relatives here at that time."

JANE

San Carlos River

1997

"There were so many animals that came to the river back then," Jane said. "The San Carlos has been giving them food and water for hundreds of years."

A few feet away, Vince saw a deer
drinking from the river. "It still does. The
river hasn't changed. That's amazing. I
wonder why the river hasn't changed."

A message popped up on Jane's screen from May 5, 1997. It said, "Help us save the river! Lina and Al." The words kept flashing on the screen.

"Jane, we have to do something!" said Vince. "Since you and I can travel back in time, let's go back and help them."

Jane agreed that they should travel back into the past and see the river as it was back in 1997.

Jane sent a message to get the time machine. Suddenly the Time Traveler, a big bubble ship, floated down to the ground. "Get ready for a trip, Jane. Let's travel back in time to the year 1997," said Vince.

"If we go back, we can't change things ourselves," Jane reminded him. "We can only help Lina and Al."

Vince said, "I know, but let's try to help them." Vince and Jane changed into 1997 clothes and got into the Time Traveler. Then it rose into the sky and began its journey back in time.

Vince and Jane to the Rescue

The Time Traveler landed by some homes near the San Carlos River. But the year was 1997! Vince and Jane heard some voices outside. They peeked out and saw a girl and a boy talking to a woman. Jane quickly did a computer check on them. "It's Lina and Al!" Jane said.

The woman was saying, "I don't agree with you. I don't want to give up my green grass and flowers. I don't want to see dried up grass when I look at my yard!"

Lina said, "Mom, if we use too much water, the San Carlos River could dry up someday." Lina's mom pointed the hose at her car to wash it.

Al pointed to some bags of lawn food. He asked, "Mrs. Reyna, are you going to put all that on your lawn?"

"Yes, green grass needs lots of food and water," Lina's mom said. "It doesn't grow on its own. I'm just trying to make our home look beautiful. Don't worry so much. Nothing bad is going to happen to the river."

"But the lawn food goes into the ground, and it ends up in the river," Al said.

"And the soapy water from the car ends up in the river, too," Lina said.

"What do you want me to do?" Lina's mom asked. "Drive a dirty car? Kill the grass? Let the weeds grow? I really don't think I'm polluting the river."

"We could take our car to a car wash that uses very little water," Lina said. "And our lawn doesn't need tons of water either, Mom."

"You're our mayor," Al added. "People will listen to you if you ask them to start SAVING water."

"You could ask people to work to keep the river clean," said Lina.

Mrs. Reyna aimed the hose at her car. "I'll think about it. You two go and play. Have some fun."

Lina and Al left and started walking down the sidewalk. Vince and Jane ran to catch them. They knew no one would understand that they had come from the future. So they had to act like they were from 1997. Vince said, "Hi. We got the message you sent about saving the river."

"How did you get it?" asked Al.

"We saw it on our computer. We want to help you save the San Carlos River," Vince added. "How can we help you?"

Lina shook her head. "Thanks, but I don't know. We're having a hard time getting people to listen to us. They can't see what they're doing to the river."

"What if people could see what they are doing to the river?" asked Vince. "They may not believe you now, but we could show them proof. Let's get some water from the river and put it in these jars. Then anyone will be able to see that the river water is dirty. We'll take the jars to a TV station. We can ask if they'll do a news story about the river."

"Wow, then people really will see what they're doing to the river. This idea might work," said Lina and Al.

"Then we could ask people to call the mayor with ideas about saving the river," Vince added.

"She's my mom," Lina said. "We're trying to think of a way to get her to change her mind. She thinks nothing bad will happen to the river."

"If enough people call, maybe she'll change her mind," said Vince. "It's worth a try."

They ran to the river with the jars. Vince filled them with some dirty river water. Then he put the lids on tightly.

The Mayor's Turn

Mayor Reyna was working in her office at the city hall. People had been calling her all morning. Jim Reed from the TV station was coming to talk to her.

Someone had put a jar of dirty water on her desk. Mayor Reyna held the jar up to the light and looked at the dirty water. The label on the jar said, "San Carlos River."

The mayor's aide, Bev, walked into the office. "Did you see this article in the newspaper today? It's about how dirty the water is in the San Carlos River. Everybody wants to talk to you about it," Bev said.

"Good," the mayor said with a smile. "I have a lot to say about it. Call the newspapers and the TV stations. Call Lina and Al, too. Ask them to come over. They'll be surprised at what I have to say."

SAN CARLOS TIMES

RIVER WATER UNSAFE?

San Carlos
River

POLLUTION
PROBLEM

MAYOR REYNA

Many people came into the mayor's office. Mayor Reyna held up the jar of dirty water. "This is water from the San Carlos River. Would you drink this water? Would you swim in it? We must stop polluting this river now."

The mayor went on, "This is what we need to do. We'll do three things:

1. Conserve our water.
2. Stop polluting.
3. Learn to take care of the river.

I'm sure I can count on all of you to help save the river." Everyone clapped after the mayor's speech.

Vince and Jane said good-bye to Lina and Al. Then they sneaked back to the Time Traveler. It was time to go back to the future, to the year 2097. Vince said, "I'll miss Lina and Al. I think we helped them at just the right time."

Suddenly, a message trailed across Jane's screen. It said, "WE DID IT! Lina and Al."

Kissin